Beyond the Shadows
Exploring the Ghosts of Franklin County

Dan Terry

Copyright 2007 Missouri Kid Press

ISBN13: 978-0-9797654-2-1
ISBN: 0-9797654-2-0

Missouri Kid Press
P. O. Box 111
Stanton, Missouri 63079

Table of Contents

About the Author..iv

Foreword...v

Introduction..vi

One:		Franklin County...1
		"in the daylight, in the darkness"

Two:		New Haven..7
		"a hauntingly good time"

Three:		Berger..15
		"a town with a past that won't go away"

Four:		Enoch's Knob Bridge...27
		"urban legends run wild"

Five:		Union...31
		"a haunted house can change a man's life"

Six:		Gray Summit..35
		"diner of the damned"

Seven		Sullivan...41
		"a place of legends"

Eight		More Shadows to explore..47
		"No matter where you go, there they are"

About the Author

Dan Terry is a Franklin County native. One of four children of Virgil and Ellen Terry of Stanton, he was born in 1963 and, like many area youths, worked as a tour guide at Meramec Caverns. He attended the public school at Stanton and, in 1981, graduated from Sullivan High School, where he participated in speech and theatre and advanced to state competition.

After a four-year stint in the U.S. Coast Guard, he began a career in law enforcement, working in Franklin, Crawford and Gasconade counties. Terry has been a Police Chief and Firearms Instructor, trained by the Missouri State Highway Patrol and the FBI as well as the NRA.

To prepare for a career in law enforcement, Terry completed the 120-hour basic police course in 1986, the updated 470-hour course in 1998, and a 130-hour upgrade course in 2003. He has earned a Class A license, which qualifies him to work anywhere in Missouri. At present, he is enrolled in a course in police administration at East Central College and has completed other college work in the field of law enforcement.

In 1995, Dan went to work for the New Haven Police Dept., and was promoted to Assistant Chief of Police in 2006. Later that year, he was given the Medal of Honor for pulling a wounded deputy out of the line of fire during a gunfight.

After writing a newspaper article about local haunted spots in 1995, he founded Spookstalkers, a ghost-hunting group relying on scientific equipment over psychic impressions. This team has been on numerous investigations, including homes and businesses, and was recently asked to assist a new group investigating a ghost-infested airplane museum in Wichita, Kan. Dan's articles have also been published in *Haunted Times magazine* and in *Guns and Weapons for Law Enforcement*.

Terry makes his home in New Haven, where he lives with his wife, Sherri, a son, Brendan, two step-daughters, Amber and Natasha, and a 100-pound German shepherd who believes he's a lap dog.

Sue Blesi. Publisher

Foreword

Dan and I go back a couple of decades. We once wore the same uniform and badge when he was my Chief of Police. My path led me away from public service, but Dan is still serving others as Assistant Police Chief at New Haven.

Whatever his title, and whatever accolades he has achieved, I know from experience that Dan only wanted one title. He wanted to be known as a good cop.

His willingness to seek out truth is what makes him a good cop and a good paranormal investigator.

In the pages that follow, you will read some stories that may sound fantastic. Indeed, they are fantastic but they are also true. Truth is a way of life for some people and Dan Terry is one of these.

This I know from experience because whether we were kicking down a door with weapons drawn or crawling through a basement with electromagnetic field detectors looking for the paranormal, Dan has always acted with calm, forethought and purpose.

In this life you are lucky to find a friend who enjoys a sense of adventure and is willing to go places where only ghosts, rats and spiders haunt, and is still able to maintain his composure and invoke common sense. I have such a friend and he has written this book.

Enjoy it and know that everything he has written is true. No one has all the answers, but the quest for truth goes on.

                Samuel Tyree
                Founder, Great Plains Paranormal
                June 22, 2007
                Wichita, Kansas

Introduction
Ghosts: friends, foes, or both?

Who, in our generation, has not sat at the knee of a parent, grandparent, or other older family member and heard the family ghost stories?

I spent many sleepless nights as a child after hearing stories of phantom trains, horses, and ghosts in the attic. I still think Dad used the attic ghost to keep me in my room at night.

My first encounter with the unknown was as a child in Stanton, Mo. Our house had no air conditioning. Summer nights in Missouri can be long and hot, with sleep coming in short naps through the night. I slept in the living room because it was cooler than my bedroom and each night I heard the footsteps of someone, possibly with a wooden leg or wooden shoes, making a clip-clop sound as they approached the front door. The knob would jiggle as if someone was checking to see if it was locked, then the sound would retreat.

Three cousins from Chicago came down and spent the night on the floor with me, and they also heard the sound. They believed it was some sort of law enforcement, checking doors at night. However, Stanton was not incorporated and had no law enforcement, unless you count the single deputy sheriff who had to patrol the entire county, an area encompassing approximately 922 square miles. He hardly had time to check doors.

The original ghost buster, Kolchack, the night stalker, turned me into a ghost hunter. That show motivated me to look beyond the veil separating us from the other side. Without the fancy gadgets and tools used by the ghost hunters of today, my friends and I went out and looked to be scared.

A military tour and a career in police work, along with a family, slowed my ghost hunting down. I began going on ghost tours back in the late 90's, and after writing an article on area ghosts for a local newspaper in 2005, I started my own ghost hunting group, called Spookstalker.

Following are some of the adventures I've had, along with some haunted places in Franklin County I have not had the privilege of investigating yet. What has been reported here is the truth. Many times there were witnesses, all different in each case, to verify what I have claimed. Take it for what you will.

Before you start this journey, there are a few definitions you'll need to know. Instead of explaining the terms in each chapter, they are listed here because the reader may need to refer back to them later.

- Apparition: A ghost that looks like a person. Sometimes they are just an outline, or with a misty appearance. Sometimes they look like a full person.
- Orb: An unexplained ball of energy in photos, sometimes seen by the naked eye. Some may be dust or moisture, but many, I believe, are some sort of paranormal energy.
- EMF Detector: These are electrical devices used to detect electromagnetic fields. Sometimes these fields, which have no reason to be there, may be ghosts preparing to manifest themselves in some way.
- EVP or Electronic Voice Phenomena: Using a recorder, you can hear voices, possibly from the dead, which you could not hear at the time they were recorded.
- Shadow Person: For me, these present the biggest mystery. We don't know if they are ghosts, demons, or something else. They can be human-shaped or just a blob.

Steven LaChance, founder of Missouri Paranormal Research, told me once that there are enough haunted places in Franklin County to keep four groups busy. I have to agree. Some of the places mentioned here can be checked out without obtaining permission. Enoch's Knob Bridge, St. Johns Cemetery and others are public land. Feel free to do so. Permission will be needed to check out sites on private property.

Keep a skeptical mind, but not a closed one. Good hunting!

Drawing by Jim Peters

The old Newport Hotel, built in 1828, faces Highway 100. Recently restored, it may be the oldest building in the county

Chapter 1
Franklin County, Missouri in the daylight

Starting as a wonderland filled with American Indians, wildlife and natural forest, Franklin County is now one of the largest counties in Missouri.

The first known settler is believed to have been William Hughes, who set up his home on DuBois Creek in 1794. One year later, Daniel Boone's son, Nathan, built his homestead across the Missouri River in St. Charles County. Daniel Boone led many families from Kentucky, Tennessee and Virginia to this part of Missouri. Indian troubles on the north side of the river caused many families to migrate across the river to what is now Franklin County.

Among the early settlers were John Colter and "Wild Irish" Bob Fraizer, both of whom had served with the Lewis and Clark expedition in 1804. In 1818, Franklin County was carved out of St. Louis County and named in honor of one of our founding fathers, Benjamin Franklin.

The first village established by white men in the newly-formed county was Newport, which was selected to be the first county seat. Newport was near the Missouri River between the present-day towns of Washington and New Haven. The seat of government was moved to Union in 1826 to a more centralized location. Lost in the mist of time, little remains of the original village. Today the unincorporated hamlet consists of a church and a handful of dwellings, but there is no commerce.

Manufacturing and tourism have long played a role in Franklin County history. Once it was home to the world's largest corn cob pipe factory, the nation's largest tent manufacturer, and one of the largest shoe and hat manufacturers, along with a large fireworks factory, but these concerns have shrunk or vanished.

Beyond the Shadows

But tourism remains. Missouri, known as the "Cave State", boasts over 6000 surveyed caves. The largest commercial cave is located in Stanton.

Meramec Caverns, deep in history, was used as shelter by Indians and bears alike. In the mid to late 1700s, French explorers took saltpeter from the cave for the manufacturing of gunpowder. During the Civil War, Union forces also set up a gunpowder plant inside the cave, which was later destroyed by a Confederate guerrilla band, commanded by William Clark Quantrill and joined by a then-unheard-of soldier named Jesse James.

James used the cave for escapes from the law during his post-war career. In the 1900s, locals held dances in the grand ballroom, using their cars for lighting. Lester Dill, a showman in the tradition of P.T. Barnum, opened the cave and began taking tours through. In 1933, he discovered the upper levels of the caverns, including the "wine table", one of the rarest of cave formations. Since then, Hollywood movies have been filmed in the cave and it boasts tens of thousands of tourists each year.

In the darkness

Franklin County has a still darker past, hidden from the billboards and web sites but still remembered in the family stories and local legends of the area.

Union, Mo. August 25, 1928. "Mrs. Eugene Gifford, 50 years old, wife of a farmer living near Eureka, St. Louis County, was arrested at her home at noon today on two indictments charging her with the murder of a man and a boy."

With that headline, Franklin County got its first serial killer. Bertha Gifford, a black-haired beauty with a penchant for great cooking and caring for the sick, had worked with her first husband, named Graham, in Hillsboro, running a hotel. After the mysterious death of Graham, Bertha married Gene Gifford and moved to Catawissa, in Franklin County.

While neighbors would drop by on occasion just before meal time for her wonderful biscuits, it took time to notice the

Photo by Marc Houseman
Bertha Gifford murdered several of her victims in this house near Catawissa. It is still standing on the old Bend Road, now known as Hwy N between Catawissa and Pacific.

---

number of people who were getting sick around her.

Bertha would care for them, but they would often die under her care.

Most folks believed she was being a good Christian. Bertha was known to visit sick friends carrying a black satchel. A Pacific druggist testified that he had sold arsenic to her, presumably to kill rats in her chicken house.

After her arrest, she confessed to the murders of two people, and was a suspect in 19 more deaths, ranging in age from two to 72.

A Franklin County grand jury charged her with the murder of 17 people. At least three bodies were exhumed, one adult and two local children. An abnormal amount of arsenic was found in their systems. Bertha claimed she was helping them with their upset stomachs.

Beyond the Shadows

While stoic in her attitude during the arrest and court hearing, she became hysterical in her cell at the Franklin County jail. Were her victims visiting her, getting their own brand of justice?

In 1928, Bertha Gifford was found not guilty by reason of insanity, and was placed in a mental health facility in Farmington, Mo., for the rest of her life. Local legend was that she became the head chef there.

During the Civil War, loyalties in Franklin County, as with the rest of Missouri, were divided. Harassment, assault and murder took place between former friends and family.

Others brought their problems to the county. The Third Mo. State Militia, fighting for the United States under the command of Maj. James Wilson, had long been a thorn in the side of the 15th Mo. Cavalry, CSA under the command of Col. Tim Reeves, a Confederate officer. Wilson's men had stopped or delayed the Confederates many times in Southern Missouri and Northern Arkansas during the war.

But, following the battle of Pilot Knob, revenge was at hand. Gen. Sterling Price's men had captured Maj. Wilson and some of his men. They turned them over to Col. Reeves, probably knowing they would not make it to a POW camp.

The men were taken to Franklin County, to the bank of St. John's Creek near the Bolte farm. On Oct. 23, locals searching for persimmons found the rotting bodies. The soldiers had been executed by multiple gunshots and left lying for the wild hogs and buzzards to feast upon.

This disgusting treatment was only to be outdone by the Union forces, who then pulled an equal number of Confederate prisoners from the POW camp near St. Louis and executed them in a twisted case of revenge. Can such atrocities bring about some of the haunting we have in the county today?

Exploring the Ghosts of Franklin County

Above: The present Franklin County Courthouse, built in 1923, has been the scene of hangings. The gallows is still intact in the ceiling of the former Franklin County Clerk's office.

The first courthouse in Union was a log structure that stood on the northeast corner of the square. Ambrose Ransom rented the building to the county.

Beyond the Shadows

Photo by Dan Terry

Doug Borgmann seated at the bar at Boondocker's in New Haven. Author Dan Terry was taking random photographs while waiting for the Cardinal baseball game to be over so they could turn off the lights and proceed with their investigation of paranormal activity. Kathy Borgman had reported that the ghost sat next to Doug at the bar every night. When the photo was developed, an orb was clearly visible near the bar.

Chapter 2

New Haven, Missouri
"a hauntingly good time"

New Haven, Mo., is a small town located on the Missouri River. On Saturday, May 16, 1804, Lewis and Clark became the first representatives of the new American government to map the area. Until then, only American Indians, animals, and a few trappers and explorers had been through the area.

One of the trappers, Philip Miller, had come to Missouri with Daniel Boone. In 1836, Miller filed ownership papers for the land, which became known as Miller's Landing. In 1881, the village was incorporated and the name was changed to New Haven.

Like many others in its day, New Haven was born by the river and the railroad. As transportation changed, the boats and the trains no longer stopped, but the construction of Highway 100 kept the community alive. Today, less than 2000 people live in New Haven, but it has factories, businesses and retail stored. In 2006, it was the fastest growing community in Franklin County.

In the seventies, a bar by the name of Boondockers was something of a fixture in the river bottomland between New Haven and Berger. The flood of 1985 destroyed the business, but not the entrepreneur spirit of the owners. They bought a former Ford dealership and turned it into a restaurant and bar, calling it Boondockers. After several changes of ownership, it is still a bar with a dance floor and restaurant.

Previous owners complained about a mischievous ghost and it is still playing games at Boondockers. The current owners, Doug and Cathy Borgmann, as well as their employees, have plenty of stories to tell. Cassie, a former waitress, has heard the ghost whistle. "And, when my hands are full," Cassie said, "it would sometimes open the door to the storeroom for me."

Cathy Borgmann also reports having heard the whistle and describes it as sounding like a farmer whistling for his dog. The first time she saw the ghost was in September 2005. "I came in early to make breakfast," Cathy said in an interview the following month. "I looked into the mirror and saw him sitting there at the bar." She described him as wearing a white shirt, with old-fashioned puffy sleeves that cinched down at the wrists. Cathy did not see his head and he disappeared as soon as she turned around.

Nothing more was heard (or seen) from the ghost until the fall of 2006 when he again became active. Cathy reported, "I was standing at the stove, stirring the sausage gravy for breakfast. I felt something behind me and looked down instead of turning around." Cathy saw, standing behind her, a pair of knee-high black boots, and tan pants. Afraid to turn around, Cathy continued to stir gravy until the legs walked away.

Cathy's husband, Doug Borgmann, has also had experiences but the ghost was not quite the gentleman for Doug that he had been for Cassie. "As I walked down the hallway with my arms loaded with Pepsi, the ghost shut the storeroom door!" Doug had heard the waitresses tell about the ghost opening the door for them. "I yelled at the ghost, telling it to knock its shit off," Borgmann said. The ghost has not opened or closed a door for him since.

But, that does not mean it has given up on teasing the owner. Doug's band, Wildcard, plays the ghost's favorite song each night. It is "Haunted House", by Bobby "Boris" Pickett. "Each time we start, we get distortion from one speaker," said Randy Klienheider, another member of the band. "We've replaced the wires, the speaker, and the equalizer, and tried moving it to different locations. But, as soon as we play "Haunted House", the distortion stops. I changed the speakers and the wires myself, trying to find the source of the distortion." According to Borgmann, no cause was ever found, and no other band has the problems.

During the summer of 2006, Doug was working in the office after closing. "I was the only person in the building, but could hear talking on the floor.

Then the ghosts started having a party of their own." He described the noise as murmuring, pops and clicks, then more mumbling. I finally had enough, and told them to enjoy themselves. "I left for the night."

Boon Armstrong, who owns a carving shop in New Haven called Boon's Woodies, is a former bartender at Boondockers. He recalled having the same problem when closing up one night while Doug was on a hunting trip. "When it started turning on the juke box, which I had shut off myself, I decided to leave for the night. When it lifted a metal ladle from above the stove and threw it on the floor, I just locked the door, leaving the money in the cash register. I had had enough!"

The same week, a new ghost made its first appearance. Cathy was again working one afternoon in the kitchen when she saw the child. "I was the only one in the building. Looking through the door, I saw a small girl, maybe four or five years old, run across the room. I thought someone had come in, so I ran in to check. There was no one inside and no one was in the parking lot."

The child was described as having long brown hair and wearing an old-fashioned print dress. That was all Cathy could see. "I got the impression she was running – playing."

Lisa Hays began working as a waitress at Boondockers in the late summer of 2006. Coming from a neighboring town, she had never heard the ghost stories. But, she did hear from the ghost. "I was working and there was no one in the dining room, then I heard a little girl talking, as if to herself. I was back in the bar, and I ran up to see who had came in. There was no one in there." Lisa also checked the building and the parking lot, but there was no one in the building with her. Lisa says she has heard the little girl several times since then, but has never found her.

Between the dining room and the bar is a heavy, oak "woodie", carved by Boone Armstrong, depicting a bearded man. It resembles a totem pole and is about four feet high and weighs over 150 pounds. One night, as Doug was closing up, the old man turned!

"I left the room, and the statue was right where it had always been. When I came out the door to the kitchen, it was turned and staring at me. I tried to turn it, and it was heavy. There is no way it could have done it by natural means." Doug left at that moment.

On Oct. 8, 2006, Cathy Borgmann walked into the barroom and made an announcement to the empty room. "I have some friends coming in. They are not going to hurt you. Please let them know you're here." With that, the first Boondocker ghost hunt began. The Borgmanns established one rule to allowing us to investigate the place. Don't anger the ghosts. As Cathy said, "I have to work here alone."

The night of the investigation, the World Series playoffs featuring the St. Louis Cardinals was on television. While Doug watched the game, Cathy informed the team of a new sighting. Two days earlier, Doug had been watching the game, just like he was doing at the time. Cathy called him into the kitchen and, as he entered, she saw over his shoulder, the familiar tan pants and black boots crossing behind Doug. Cathy says she knows the ghost sits next to Doug at the bar. Could our New Haven Horror be a Cardinal fan?

While waiting for the game to end, I began taking random photos of the room. In one of the photos, a large glowing orb was sitting at the bar, next to Doug. I attempted to immediately recreate it with the camera, in case it was a reflection on the mirror. However, I was not able to recreate the image.

I began taking EMF readings on the dance floor. The electricity had been turned off at the breaker. I suddenly got a reading, with the lights on the ELF zone detector going from safe green, bypassing yellow to danger – RED. The spot was four feet from the floor. I moved the detector a few inches in all directions, and when I returned to the spot, the energy was gone. I continued to search, finding the danger zone again six feet off the floor and a few feet to the right. Just as suddenly, it was gone again, only to be found in a different area again.

Someone took a photo while I was searching the floor for the energy reading, and the picture revealed two bright orbs over my head. The ghosts were letting me know they were there.

When the game was over, we shut down the lights and began taking EVPs. All of the investigators, as well as Cathy and Doug, could hear a mumbling near the pool tables. These sounds came through on the digital recorder, unintelligible but recognizable as mumbling. Also during this time, small flashes of light could be seen on the dance floor around one of the investigators who was sitting on the floor speaking to the ghosts. There were no windows in this section of the bar so there was no way for light to reflect into the room.

While I was sitting on the floor, I saw a human-shaped shadow near the bar. I asked if anyone else noticed the shadow, and as investigator/skeptic Frank Garren turned, the shadow ran down the length of the bar, turning right at a perfect 90-degree angle, and disappeared into the dining room. Video cameras there failed to pick up the shadow.

The investigation moved into the dining room. As we began speaking for EVPs, several noticed a candle shaking at odd times. Candles had been set up to provide light for the video recorder. Doug Borgmann made the statement that the candle was answering me. To be sure it was not a trick of air currents, another candle was placed on the table next to the first one. It did not flicker at all while the other candle went wild on certain questions.

Believing the candle shook violently for yes, I asked it I was speaking to the ghost of the small girl. Getting a yes answer, I continued to ask questions about the other ghosts, sometimes asking the same questions again and getting the same response.

While asking questions, I gleaned the following information:

1. There are a total of five ghosts in the building.
2. The male ghost is protecting her, but she does not know him.
3. She is afraid of one of the other ghosts, but not of us.

Beyond the Shadows

All the male investigators had observed that, whenever we attempted to speak to the child while in the dance room, we would get a chill. The women never felt this, and at one time I observed, with my digital thermometer, a seven degree instant drop while talking to the child. The only time a female felt the cold chill was when investigator Sherri Terry made the statement "What are you going to do when I take the little girl home with me?" Then, she felt the chill.

During the discussion with the candle, I asked the question, "Were you killed by a car?" Immediately after that, Sherri asked, "Did you die before cars?" A later check showed the only clear EVP of the night was a raspy male voice saying, "Yes."

Two events occurred at Boondockers in 2007. Officer Meg Parks, a 10-year law enforcement veteran, experienced two separate incidents there. One night, on a midnight shift, a skeptical Parks made the statement outside the closed bar, "If you're really there, prove it." At that time, a light turned on outside the building for the first time. Parks did not challenge the ghost again.

Later, while approaching the restroom, Parks observed that the closet door between the restrooms opened as she approached, just as Cassie and other waitresses had reported. There was no one inside, and there were no windows or vents.

Unable to sleep, investigator Frank Garren went to get gas for his wife's vehicle at 3:30 A.M. As he passed the bar, he observed an interior light coming on and going off. He watched it for several minutes, observed that there were no vehicles in the parking lot, then knocked on the door loudly. The lights ceased shutting on and off, and he watched another 30 minutes. A check with the owners later indicated this was impossible because the lights had been shut off at the breaker.

Whatever spirit or spirits are haunting Boondockers, they still seem to be friendly and helpful, if not comical. Doug believes at least one of the spirits is protecting Cathy and he appreciates this.

In May 2007, two more ghosts made their appearance. The first, a small boy, made a splash by scaring two young girls, ages 4 and 6.

The two girls had told their families that they had been talking to a small boy in the hallway. A short time later, the two girls came screaming out of the hallway and climbed into the laps of family members. The next day, they calmed down enough to say that the boy had come at them, through the wall and through the gumball machines!!

The next week, Kathy saw an adult woman near the pool tables, where the mumbling had been heard. The spirit was described as wearing a flower print dress similar to the dress the small girl had been wearing when Kathy had seen her the previous year. Her hair was pulled back. She smiled before disappearing into thin air between the tables. Could this be the grown-up child that Kathy saw before?

If you stop in for the famous fried chicken on Wednesday, or for a burger on Friday, and the bathroom door opens for you as you approach, don't scream. Just thank the spirit and remember to leave a tip.

"The spirits that I summoned up I now can't rid myself of."
-Johann Wolfgang von Goethe in the "Sorcerer's Apprentice, 1797"

Beyond the Shadows

Loretta Cofffman of New Haven holds an EMF detector at St. John's Cemetery on Highway B in Berger. The detector would flash and beep in response to questions -- a sign of paranormal activity. The globe in the background is not the moon. It is an orb.

Chapter 3

Haunted Berger
"a town with a past that won't go away"

At one time called the "biggest and busiest unincorporated place in Franklin County", Berger was one of the earliest settlements. Originally called Big Bottoms, the Phillip Brothers were among the first settlers, arriving in 1805. Like most of the villages along the Missouri River, Berger began to grow with the coming of the railroad. Berger was laid out as a town on June 6, 1870, and at that time boasted two dry good stores, a blacksmith and wagon shop, saddle shop, hotel, brickyard, three churches and at least one bar.

The Old Berger Saloon was established in 1868 by Daniel Haid, Sr. It operated as a saloon from 1868 until 2003, when it was purchased by the current owners and made into a convenience store.

How many traumatic events can occur in a bar nearly 140 years old? One of the more recent events occurred on March 17, 1986. Jack Schaefer, age 38, had received an order of protection to stay away from his girlfriend and her children, who lived in an upstairs apartment over what was then called Mac's Café. In an effort to convince her of his undying love, Jack phoned in a bomb threat to her place of employment. He had previously been charged and convicted of making bomb threats.

That was the final straw. Jack sat in Mac's Café and drank. After a while, the spurned lover, intoxicated and angry, went into Berger bottoms and began shooting a shotgun into the air and at the sand piles. Franklin County deputies were on the way when Jack decided to make the ultimate sacrifice to love by murdering his ex.

Jack went to the apartment and attempted to kick the door open. Unable to accomplish this, he went outside to Market Street and shot out the windows of the apartment as his ex and her children hid in fear. Unable to get a response, Schaefer returned to the upstairs apartment and, using the shotgun as a universal key, shot the lock off the door.

Inside the apartment, instead of a group of victims waiting to die, Schaefer found her 19-year-old son, John, with a shotgun of his own. John fired, nearly decapitating Jack Schaefer instantly.

While Jack Schaefer's physical body was removed from the building, his soul was not. Zena Gardner, daughter of the former owner and former employee of the bar, remembered seeing his ghost in the corner of the bar several times -- always wearing the same clothes he was killed in: flannel shirt, jeans and work boots. He, reportedly, has been seen by several customers and employees, always hanging around the dark corner, forever watching the kind of celebration he is never again allowed to join.

On Aug. 19, 2001, another spurned lover sat at Mac's drinking to forget his troubles. Dennis Purdy, 41, had returned from work on a river barge and discovered his estranged wife, Lori Ann Purdy, had a new boyfriend. Lori, 27, was an employee at Mac's Café, and had been in fear for her life for some time. Lori had filed for divorce, and had gotten a temporary order of protection against Dennis. That order was issued on June 25, but had been dropped on July 2 when neither Dennis nor Lori showed up for the hearing. Friends say Lori was afraid to go through with the full order of protection, fearing Dennis would kill her as he had threatened many times before. Dennis's own brother helped her to get a home in nearby New Haven to get away from him. New Haven is the closest town with a full time police department to help protect her. However, she had moved back to Berger with a new boyfriend. Dennis and Lori's on-again-off-again romance would end that day for good.

Purdy heard that Lori had gone out with another man for a day of floating. Michael Begemann was a former soldier and worked as a mechanic. At 8:50 P.M., Dennis Purdy went to the residence of Begemann. In a strange repeat of a night 14 years earlier, Dennis carried a shotgun to finish the day. He walked around the house to where Mike was cleaning the day's catch of fish. A shotgun blast ended Mike's mechanic career. Purdy went inside to find Lori attempting to hide. Lori Ann was killed by a shotgun blast to the face. After killing his love, Purdy turned the gun on himself and pulled the trigger, avoiding a lengthy court trial.

One more event made an indelible mark on that location. Just after New Years, on a Thursday night in January 1979, two children died in a house fire. The two-story house was adjacent to Mac's Café. The Combs family lived on the first floor and their married daughter and her family lived upstairs.

An electric space heater overheated, causing a fire on that cold morning while the parents were away at work. Killed were 12-year-old Donny Sterba and his eight-year-old brother, Butch. Both died of smoke inhalation. Four other children were rescued.

With this much trauma in such a short time, how much more has happened over the past 140 years that was never reported, or never written about? Is it any wonder the ghosts have not left Berger?

I spoke with one of the residents of the upstairs apartment of Mac's Cafe in September 2005. Wendi Busch, a single mom raising her children, had plenty to say.

"Ghosts?" Wendi asked when I told her the reason I wanted to interview her. "Oh, my God! That apartment is so weird!"

Wendi spoke of leaving all the lights on when she left only to discover that the lights were all off when she returned. Many times, she and her roommate left for several hours, with Wendi having the only key and the door locked, only to return and find the shower running. But, the best story is yet to come…

"One night, my roommate and I left. We were gone a few hours, leaving the lights on and the TV off. The kids were with their father and I had the only key.

"When we returned, the lights were off, even though the door was still locked. But the weird thing is the TV and VCR were on, and The Exorcist was playing. Dan, we don't own The Exorcist!!"

Wendi did not know where the tape came from or who put it in the VCR. "I still have the tape," Wendi said. "I never did find the box, and no one ever claimed it." She struggles for a rational explanation. And she still has never watched the movie. "I don't believe in ghosts," Wendi said. "If I did, I couldn't go home at night."

At the time of the original interview, the owners of the building and business were reluctant to be known as a haunted place. Two years later, they were ready to discuss their own ghosts.

Darlene had always been interested in ghosts. Now, things were getting weird.

"I'm okay, as long as the lights are on," she said. "if the lights go out, like a power outage, I am out of here! They start moving things, and playing games, making noise. Herb doesn't like to even come in here at night."

Darlene went on to say her tenants upstairs, new ones since my interview with Wendi, were beginning to notice things.

"A few weeks ago, they called about an odor in the stairway." Darlene told me. "Herb came in and he could smell it too. It was horrible! We searched all over the place for a dead animal, but couldn't find anything. The strange part was, you could not smell it anywhere except that one small spot. Not behind the stairs, not in the next room, not up the stairs. Just there."

The odor went away by itself a few hours later. Not normal for a dead animal. It did reappear a few days later. . . . on the front porch of another alleged haunted house down the street!

Darlene had seen someone standing by her shoulder in the office, disappearing when she turned her head. Both Darlene and Herb said every night, when closing the office, they just knew there was someone still inside the small room, ready to jerk the door out of their hands. Herb said he would only work on the building after dark if it was absolutely necessary and, even then, he got done as quickly as possible. And the ghost always got active around 9:00 P.M., when they closed for the night.

On Tuesday, April 3, Spookstalker went in to investigate.

Darlene and Herb were present, along with their daughter, Tina, and her friend, Ashley. Frank Garren and I were there on behalf of Spookstalker. We began our investigation in the basement where Tina and Darlene both felt uneasy.

Darlene said that sometimes, even with the lights on in the basement, it looked completely dark when she went down there. You actually have to be in line of sight with a bulb to see the light there. Tina had also experienced this and said it had happened to her and Ashley earlier that day.

As we went down the stairway to the basement, I also noticed the darkness was different from most places. It did seem completely dark until we got to the bottom of the stairs, where you could see the 100-watt bulb in the corner. The air seemed oppressive as if the humidity was heavier there.

I began speaking to the spirit, attempting to get an EVP. Frank was investigating a small room under the stairs when he exclaimed loudly about a horrible smell under the stairs. Tina and Ashley went immediately to his side and they also noticed the odor. Just as suddenly, the odor disappeared, leaving only a normal basement musty smell. Tina and Frank both described it as a musky smell, with an overtone of what Frank described as methane or sulfur.

We began finding cold spots in the basement, changing temperature by several degrees. Frank went upstairs to get the digital thermometer, which we had left in the equipment bag. While he was gone, I asked the ghost if he was afraid of us.

Almost instantly, Tina and Ashley, both standing across the room from me, began to gag. Tina ran across the room with her hand across her mouth, as Ashley turned her face away and made gagging noises. Both said the same smell, just as described by Herb as being in the stairway a few weeks before, had appeared between the two girls making them sick. The smell dissipated as quickly as it came. At another point, Frank mentioned the nickname of the 19-year-old who had pulled the trigger on Jack over 21 years earlier. When Frank said "John-John", there was a sudden loud noise as if someone had jumped from the top of the stairs to the center, which caused the staircase

Beyond the Shadows

to shake violently. No one was near the stairs at that time.

The one good photograph we got there was in the basement. A random photo showed a white, thick substance floating inside an upside-down red plastic milk crate. It was not visible to us at the time, nor was it caused by anything inside the crate. Could it have been one of the children playing hide and seek?

We went upstairs for two hours, and observed a state liquor license, framed and displayed along with other licenses on the wall behind the cash register, begin swinging. We also observed movement inside the small, windowless kitchen, and heard other sounds. Tina noticed a cold spot next to her, and picked up the digital thermometer, which indicated a drop of 18 degrees. When she called me over, both Darlene and Herb noticed the cold "breeze" as it passed away from me and into a wall. Later, we went back into the basement, this time the feeling was normal. There was no heavy humidity. The light was obvious when we opened the door to the steps. Darlene and Tina both said the spirits had left. Spookstalker was invited to come back for an all-night investigation.

"You have to talk to Andy," Sam told me. "Just ask him about his apartment in Berger." Samantha Menke was an employee at the local gas station, and I had known her and Andy since they were both ten years old.

Andy is the type of midwestern corn-fed young man typical of rural Missouri. Big and strong with a heart to match, Andy is as down to earth as they come. Surely, he was not the type to believe in ghosts.

But, Sam was convincing. I met up with Andy one night while he and his pregnant girlfriend, Star, were climbing into the car. I asked Andy about a rumor I had heard about him living in a haunted place.

Andy just looked at me, like looking at a new species of bug. Then, voice somewhat cracking, said "Are you going to make fun of me?"

This was an answer I had never encountered before. I explained that I was working on a book about ghosts and was particularly interested in Berger and had seen some weird things myself. Andy relaxed slightly, and said only this:

"We used to hear voices, laughing and joking, on the steps. But, the steps were against an outside wall. One time, Star was yelling at me because she heard me in the room with her, and she was mad at me anyway, but I was downstairs. Then . . . "

Andy looked away, towards Star who was sitting in their car. He seemed reluctant to continue.

"Dan, I've read the Bible, and I know what devils are. But my baby is overdue, and I just don't want to talk about it now."

I have tried to talk to Andy about it since then, but each time he says he hasn't forgotten, and we'll do it soon. I stopped bringing it up, believing that whatever happened there, it bothers him to speak of it.

Later, I spoke to the current resident of the same apartment. The building is a stone block building, probably dating back to the 1930s. The current resident declined to speak about it except to say he had been told by Andy about the place prior to moving in. For a while, he also noticed the odd noises until he decided that the stories of a 19-year-old kid were not going to scare him out of his home. Since then, he has ignored it.

During the investigation at Darlene's, another potential place was pointed out to us. A former hotel, built in the late 19th century, was one block down and had been empty for seven years. Since purchasing the old Mac's Café, Darlene had seen some weird stuff at the old hotel.

"Since I've been here," Darlene reported, "When the power goes out all over town, there are always lights in that old building although the electricity had been cut off at the pole!"

Built in 1878 and named the Hall Hotel, the building has been a hotel, train station, bar, private residence, a dentist office in the back, and for a short time a brothel. It contains nine bedrooms, and one room with a decorative tin ceiling which, reportedly, was the "bathroom", where patrons could pay for a hot bath. Heated water was brought up from downstairs and poured into tubs.

Darlene reported that she and her husband had seen a

male figure walking on the front porch, before disappearing. And the strange smell that Herb had checked on in their stairway had moved to the front porch of the Hall Hotel the following day, remaining for several hours before dissipating.

Darlene had spoken to the new resident of the house, Rob Hudson. Rob lived there with his girlfriend, her children, and his own boys on weekends. That is, until his boys refused to visit because the "house was haunted." Now, they stay up the street with a grandparent and visit Rob only during daylight.

I spoke with Rob, who reported his eighteen-month-old child had been staring at something up the stairs then screamed and ran to him. All members of the family, including the dog, had seen a shadow as it walked past their rooms almost every night, approaching the stairway. Rob also confirmed that the strange odor had moved from Darlene's to his residence, and he had heard strange knocking noises. He mentioned that one room in the basement gives him the feeling of being watched, and he tends to ignore it. At this time, Rob was doing his best to ignore it, as moving was too expensive. I suggested that one day, when passing through New Haven, Rob contact me for more information and we'd set up a date for an investigation.

Then, on Sunday, April 22 at 8:40 P.M., I received the most unusual call of my ghost hunting career.

"Dan, this is Rob. -- Hudson, from Berger." I could hear the panic in his voice. "You remember the ghost thing? Well, tonight it attacked me!"

Rob went on to say that he had been putting in a hot water heater in the basement. After the person helping him left, he went downstairs to relieve pressure on the water heater, when a sheet of plastic, weighed down with boards and used to keep the heat on the pipes, suddenly leaped straight up near his face, as if attempting to choke him. Rob ran up the stairs, and after calming down somewhat he called me.

Since he refused to go back into the basement until I arrived, we made plans to meet on Monday night for a preliminary check. Then, we planned an investigation for the following Friday night.

On Monday, April 23 at 6:30 P.M., I met with two members of the team, Jamie and Loretta. We met with Rob and discussed the history of the building and the current problems. A check of the area revealed there were two cisterns on the property, one in the house and one just outside. An exterior wall, a relatively new addition, was built over part of the outside cistern. Cisterns have long been suspected as being a supernatural portal. The cistern in the residence was less than three feet from the sheet of plastic that attacked Rob.

Research revealed that a man named John had lived there with his wife, Mabel, and their mentally challenged son, John James. John had died in the house, lying on a bed in the living room with the upstairs shut off by sheets of plastic to help hold the heat downstairs. After his death, his wife and son continued to live there for several years until Family Services stepped in. Mabel had been sinking deeper into dementia and John James was ill equipped to take care of the ramshackle old building. John James, working at the local sheltered workshop, was moved to his own apartment and Mabel was moved into a home, where she died just last year.

Other than a few orbs, we obtained very little evidence. There were three kids, a mother, and a dog playing upstairs while we searched downstairs. After a tour of the house and a short EVP investigation, we left for the night.

On Friday, the three of us returned with two video cameras and we had an empty house all to ourselves. Rob remained with us but everyone else had left for the evening. The one room where Rob said he felt watched was the main target. This room had yielded our best orbs on our previous visit, and there was a strange shadow with no explanation on the wall behind one of the investigators. When I began speaking, calling John by name and informing him I knew John James, I felt a stronger feeling of someone behind me than I had ever felt before. A photo taken at that second showed a very large orb behind me.

Beyond the Shadows

Later analysis of the photos showed some interesting reflections in glass. In the upstairs window, three photos showed what appeared to be a hooded figure watching us. In the same room, another window showed what appeared to be a very unhappy male spirit watching us. Downstairs, on the television screen, which was shut off at the time, a reflection showed a distorted figure with large eyes.

Research done by Loretta and Jamie showed that Silas Hall built both the Hall Hotel and, after a fire destroyed the original bar which was located where Darlene's One Stop is now, Hall bought the land and built the current building.

During this investigation, we also got some pink orbs in the room of a little girl. Video obtained nothing. I instructed the spirits to remain in the basement and not to cause fear or harm to the people in the residence. As of this writing, Rob has had nothing further to report.

The team did an investigation at St. John's Cemetery, which is located on Highway B entering into Berger. Famous for ghostly activity, neighbors have even called the police, believing vandals were damaging the graves.

Aside from orbs, we received flashing lights on an EMF detector, which led us to one particular grave. Loretta was speaking to the spirit, and on occasion it seemed to answer her by causing the detector to flash. After several minutes of no contact, Loretta made the statement that she was leaving if the spirit has stopped. At that moment, the EMF detector flashed four times in rapid succession: it wasn't ready to be alone.

Checking the photos taken from different angles by Jamie and myself, we found there was always an orb around Loretta's head -- sometimes faded, sometimes glowing brightly, but always near her.

Stop by St. John's Cemetery on a dark night. Say hello, but I'd refuse any invitation to spend the night. I'm not sure just how lonely the spirits may be or how desperate they may be for company!

Exploring the Ghosts of Franklin County

Photo by Jamie Eckerle

Spookstalker founder and paranormal investigator Dan Terry felt a tingle on his neck during a paranormal Investigation in the basement of the old Hall Hotel in Berger. Terry had been calling the ghost by name and received no response until he called the name of the ghost's son. He felt something behind him and asked another investigator to take a picture. The orbs shown above his head and behind him revealed the presence he had sensed.

Beyond the Shadows

Enoch's Knob Bridge southeast of New Haven has been the scene of at least two deaths in recent years and numerous reports of paranormal activity. There are unconfirmed rumors of early tragedies at the site.

Chapter 4

Enoch's Knob Bridge
"urban legends run wild"

The old bridge yet stands despite nature's best attacks. Rusty metal beams and a rotting wood floor compete with Boeuf Creek below eroding the banks. Yearly floods clean out the beer cans and trash dumped off the bridge by local party-goers. Legends about the bridge are much more colorful than the facts.

Stories include ghost dogs barking, demon dogs appearing on the bridge with green eyes and three legs; trolls in the woods, tree spirits and ghosts, lovelorn teens hanging themselves on the bridge, or throwing themselves to the jagged rocks below.

Research indicates two deaths connected with the area. One of these spirits is reported to be the ghost of Enoch's Knob Bridge.

On August 23, 1987, a young man named Patrick Kinneson was attending a party on the bridge. Recovering from a broken hip, he, reportedly, remained alone while his friends went to help push a vehicle stuck in the mud of a corn field.

No one saw Kinneson climb the rusty girders. And no one saw him fall to his death on the rocks 37 feet below. His body was found some time later that night. He was pronounced dead there that night, and the death was ruled accidental.

Since then, reports of red eyes glowing, demon dogs and monsters in the woods have been filed. People who remember Kinneson say he was a practical joker, and some believe he is still there playing games.

The other death occurred on May 9, 2005. Stephen Cooksey, 41, was killed during a drug transaction. Despite multiple shots with a .22 caliber rifle, he managed to drag himself under his vehicle.

Beyond the Shadows

That car was later set on fire by the killers, burning the body. While no ghosts have been attributed to him, perhaps Kinneson has company. One deputy, who will remain nameless to avoid teasing by other deputies, assisted in the investigation of the homicide. He told me that several months later, while crossing the bridge, every electrical device in his vehicle except the radio shut off. The engine died and the vehicle coasted across the bridge. Once on the other side, it started quickly. The deputy told me he would never go out there again without a call. No more routine patrols on the devil's bridge.

So who did we talk to the night Spookstalker went to visit? On Saturday, May 13, 2007, Loretta, Jamie and I went to investigate the famous bridge, possibly the most investigated haunted scene in the county. We arrived, and I walked to the bridge with the camera while the two girls finished getting the cameras and recorders working. Strangely enough, the cameras stopped functioning for a short time. Later, on the recorders, you can hear the girls complaining of the cameras not working. Then, a male voice in that monotone usually heard in EVPs, says "Go to Hell."

The only other EVP we got that night was while I was asking the spirits to come around me while we took pictures. Many times, this has worked to get something when nothing else was happening. This time, the digital recorder taped my voice asking "Pat" to come by me for the picture. Again, the camera stopped working. Then, my voice can be heard making the statement to photograph my hand, as I had just felt something touch me. What I had felt was like a spider web going across the back of my hand.

Later, we heard the same voice as before, right after my request for Pat to stand next to me. It asked, "Why?" Then, I felt the touch. Did Pat attempt to shake hands? Or was it Stephen? Go out and try to talk to him. Some still say if you turn off the lights and honk three times, you'll see the demon dog with the glowing eyes. Go ahead, but I think you'll get more results from talking with Pat.

"... And when your children's children think they are alone in the fields, the forests, the shops, the highways, or the quiet of the woods, they will not be alone. There is no place in this country where a man can be alone. At night when the streets of your towns and cities are quiet, and you think they are empty, they will throng with the returning spirits that once thronged them, and that still love these places."
-- Chief Seattle in a speech to the governor of Washington Territory, ca. 1855.

Beyond the Shadows

The "screaming house" of Union has attained nationwide attention when the story was aired on the Discovery Channel. The photo is a postcard photo of Cedar Street in 1912.

Chapter 5

Union, Missouri

"a haunted house can change a man's life"

Steven LaChance is quickly becoming a name in the Paranormal community. He earned his place.

Union, Mo., is the county seat of Franklin County. Founded in 1825, the name was chosen to express the coming together of ideas and people. Today, it is not only the county seat, but also the home of East Central College.

The story of the screaming house of Union has been told countless times. In 2006, Discovery Channel aired their "A Haunting" series season, opening with the story of LaChance in the episode entitled "Fear House". It was also printed in the 2006 release "Weird U.S. Presents: Weird Hauntings", and in May 2007, LaChance announced a lecture tour entitled "The Survivors Tour" with well known demonologist John Zaffis.

I had an e-mail discussion with LaChance shortly after publishing my first article on ghosts. Suddenly, all contact stopped. I later learned that LaChance was still suffering from the effects of his close call with Satan's Hordes, and for a time had attempted to exit the paranormal world. It was only when others convinced him that running away would not help him did he return to help in the fight against evil.

I will keep the location of the residence secret, respecting the owners of the house and the current occupants.

This is not my story to tell. I can relate what I have been told by LaChance. They moved into a rental house which was probably possessed by at least one demon. It not only used their own fears to attack the children and Steven, but after running the family out of the house, the spirit manifested itself as a black cloud, and was seen going from room to room searching for its victims.

After getting away from the cursed house, LaChance discovered a severe lack of professional assistance with victims of the paranormal. He then founded Missouri Paranormal Research, undoubtedly the top paranormal research group in the Midwest. Little did he know that forming this investigative committee would be a double edge sword. One of the first investigations was back in the demonic house he had left a year earlier and the demon was attacking another innocent family.

Forced back into the hell house, Steven opened himself up again to the anger and hatred of the spawn of Satan. Not only did he suffer emotional and physical attacks, but was nearly murdered when the demon emotionally forced his friend, the woman living in the residence, to come to his new home with a weapon intent upon killing him. Steven dodged that one, and eventually helped her get the spiritual help she needed. Not before, however, she was in the grips of the unholy being and showed unnatural strength while being forced into a hospital.

After assisting this family in escaping the hell on earth, LaChance and his group became famous with other investigations. I was at a ghost conference in Arkansas when Steven LaChance was tapped to speak after the scheduled guest speakers failed to show up. His genuine demeanor and inspiring story of demonic opression, fear for his children, and escape as well as the return to the pit of hell changed the man from a non-believer to a driving force in paranormal research. Look up his story, then say you don't fear the demonic. I dare you.

"Thus we play the fools with the time, and the spirits of the wise sit in the clouds and mock us."
William Shakespeare

Exploring the Ghosts of Franklin County

Photo provided by Sue Blesi

The old red covered bridge over the Bourbeuse River at Union was a spooky place for travelers at night because it was impossible to see what might be lurking inside. This bridge was later destroyed by a tornado.

Beyond the Shadows

Photo by Dan Terry

Sherri Terry and Tim Clifton challenge ghosts at Tri-County Restaurant, formerly the Old Diamonds at Gray Summit. Clifton had called to the ghosts of the murdered woman and the child to not be afraid, then he began challenging the ghost of the murderer to come out. Three orbs appeared above him that were not present in photographs that had been taken a few minutes earlier. Clifton was formerly the lead investigator with Missouri Paranormal Society and is also a Baptist minister.

Chapter 6

Gray Summit, Missouri
"diner of the damned"

Look at the long, curving walls and series of windows facing east and you can imagine just how modern The Diamonds restaurant looked in the 50s. When the dark, curvy dangerous Route 66 was the only way to transport goods across the nation, the bright lights and inviting warmth of the Diamonds must have seemed like heaven.

The Diamonds began like so many of the other cheesy tourist traps that sprouted up like mushrooms along Route 66. It started as an all-night banana shop, became a restaurant, burned, and was rebuilt into the post-modern building seen today. In a bygone era, Marilyn Monroe, Elvis Presley, and Al Capone stopped in for a respite from the road. When Interstate-44 replaced Route 66, the owners sold the building, retaining the name, and built a new Diamonds a mile away on the new highway. Now called Tri-County Truck Stop, the original structure actually outlived the new Diamonds, which closed in the 90s.

Today, the building stands empty alongside new, modern, soulless block structures housing generic truck stops with flavorless fast-food restaurants replacing the "home cooking" of yesteryear. Memories of another time can be seen everywhere, from the old style wooden phone booth to photos of some of the other tourist traps that once dotted old Route 66.

There is, however, something else at the Tri-County Truck stop that is not so pleasant – ghosts.

Stories had been floating around and were passed from employee to employee over the years. Rumors of ghosts touching employees, moving items, and whispering, were commonplace. They were never spoken of to outsiders until August 2006 when a black shadow flew up the basement stairs toward the startled workers. Then, someone called the professionals.

Missouri Paranormal Research (MPR) is a paranormal group started by Steven LaChance after his own encounter with evil forces within a rented home. His team consists of some of the most professional paranormal researchers in the St. Louis area. Due to the size of the building, MPR invited two other groups to assist, one of which was Spookstalker.

Karen Brown, former owner and current employee, told of being touched many times in the past 15 years. Karen described the touches as gentle, almost comforting, including a brush across the hair and a gentle touch of her face. Earlier this week, Karen said a customer had asked, while paying the bill, how long the restaurant had been haunted. When Karen asked why he believed that, the customer replied that while eating, the ketchup, salt and pepper had slowly slid across the table to him.

In June 2006, a small boy was on his way to the bathroom when he passed the stairway to the upstairs, which was rented out to truckers for beds and showers in the 70s. The upstairs is currently unused by the living. This child stepped from the dining room into the twilight zone.

Screaming, the child ran back into the dining room. He described a scene from a grisly movie. A man, holding a woman in front of him, suddenly slashed her throat with a knife. The child said he saw the blood gushing and ran screaming for his mother. Of course, there was no one on the stairs. However, Karen said there were dried red spots on the wall opposite the stairway and it was difficult to clean them up. No one ever figured out what the red spots were.

A waitress named Jackie mentioned that the mixer had turned itself on the day before. The door to the oven crashed open twice that week, and she heard the dish cart being pushed across the room when there was no one else in the building.

That night, members of MPR who had arrived early for supper, watched as a metal cream pitcher slowly moved across a shelf and fell to the floor. No one was behind the counter when this took place, but several patrons saw it.

Karen said the employees had named the kindly spirit "George" years ago. Laurel Brown, current owner of the business and daughter of Karen, has worked there for over 10 years. Laurel said "I've heard it call my name, rub my neck and blow on my hair. It's also spoken my name very softly. George did that to most of the employees."

Karen Brown also reported hearing her name spoken quietly and feeling the brush of her hair. What was strange about this incident was that it happened not at the Diamonds, but at the local Wal-Mart! "My husband was at the end of the aisle and there was no one near me."

Karen also told about a night when she was leaving the store. It was late at night and a young family member, as they were driving away, saw someone on the roof of the building. Karen also saw the person and returned to the building. Of course, she found no one living inside the building.

On the first night of the investigation, Greg Myers, lead investigator for MPR, took Karen Brown into the kitchen while attempting to take EVPs. When the pots and pans began clanging together, Karen ran out of the kitchen, proclaiming she had heard enough.

On this night, Spookstalker only got orbs on film. A week later, MPR returned for a follow-up investigation, and picked up evidence that has been alternately praised and condemned across the globe.

Cameras had been set up in the basement. One investigator, checking into the restroom, observed what she described as a blue flash sinking into the floor. Other investigators immediately ran downstairs to check the cameras in the basement, which had been locked down. On the film, a blue human-shaped figure could be seen walking past the camera.

This video raced through the paranormal world like a Kansas prairie fire. Many proclaimed it was a Photoshop hoax. Others praised it as true evidence. The film was shown on television news shows and Steven LaChance, founder of MPR, was interviewed on TV and radio stations around the nation.

Paranormal groups are still at odds over this video. Healthy skepticism, or jealousy?

The next investigation was equally amazing. After taking a local reporter through the basement, an old rusty knife was thrown from across the room by unseen hands, striking the metal ductwork near the investigator.

The last investigation occurred right after the restaurant closed up for good. Again, Spookstalker and MPIA was invited along. My team looked over the whole building, but settled in the basement during a lockdown. Videos taken by Spookstalker included an orb which traveled across the room, then did an immediate right angle turn and disappeared into the wall. When we were ready to leave the basement, Greg Myers stated in a loud voice "We are leaving now. If you don't show your presence, make a noise, or something, we are going to leave. Then, you'll be alone forever."

At that exact instant, every pipe in the old building -- furnace, water, and sewer -- shook violently one time! The sound was deafening in the small enclosed basement. Frank Garren, member of Spookstalker, attempted to prove this was caused by a problem with the water. He grabbed one of the pipes and pulled with all the strength of his six foot, 220 lb. frame. Nothing moved.

Sherri and I then went upstairs to investigate. This area, at one time a hotel and shower for the truckers, was used in the mid to late 70s as a haven for dopers and criminals.

That was where the psychics believed there was three spirits -- a woman, a child and a murderer! As we approached the stairs, Tim Clifton, one of the lead investigators for MPR, was coming down. Tim stopped me with words of advice:

"Dan, be careful up there." Tim said. "The murderer's spirit is up there and he is mad. I have been slapped and shoved so hard that if I had not been standing against the wall, I would have been knocked over."

We went up and began photographing. There were no orbs present at that time. I set up the recorders for EVPs, then we sat down. A short time later, Tim Clifton returned for another round with the spirit.

Tim again started challenging the spirits to show themselves. Tim asked the other two ghosts, the child and the woman, to appear. Asking if they were afraid of the third ghost, Tim began calling that ghost a coward, saying that he would only hit from the back.

During this time, I was taking random photographs. I got a photo of Tim with three bright orbs above his head and a room full of other orbs. Were the three ghosts near Tim as he had requested?

While Tim continued, I watched as a man-shaped shadow seemed to be pacing along the wall. I was looking for the source of the shadow when Tim asked if anyone else saw this. We watched the shadow for a short time then I got up and checked the windows and doors for a source. Finding nothing, I walked back to the window on the far side of the room. This one looked across the highway, and there was no trees or bushes on the second floor.

Tim said he could see both my shadow and the other one. I said, "Well, let's just block it." I then stood in front of the window, looking outside for the possibility of someone outside playing a prank. "Now what are you going to do?", I asked.

Suddenly, as if rehearsed, everyone in the room gasped. Fearing to turn around to see what was behind me, I stood by until Tim said, in a calm voice, "Dan, it's above you."

The witnesses said that when I challenged it, the shadow moved above my head. Now, the two shadows on the wall combined as one 10-foot-tall shadow. I backed off, and it resettled in its original place. Tim began challenging it to come into the room. I saw the shadow get smaller, then large again. Other witnesses swore they saw legs and arms, as if it climbed through the closed window.

The shadow then slowly disappeared and the game was over. Eighty years of history makes fact finding more difficult. Tri-County Truck Stop sits vacant now, replaced by the newer, shiner more generic truck stops, just as Route 66 was replaced by soulless Interstate 44. But, like Route 66 or the old Diamonds building, the spirits refuse to completely surrender to time or death.

Beyond the Shadows

The Harney-Hinchcliff Mansion in Sullivan originally built for Dr. Leffingwell prior to the Civil War. The mansion fell into a severe state of disrepair but the Harney Foundation is working to restore it. It was the site of a recent paranormal investigation.

Chapter 7

Sullivan, Missouri
"a place of legends"

The Gateway to the Ozarks, Sullivan had humble beginnings when Daniel Boone led his friends, Stephen and Dorcas Sullivan, to the spot now called the Meramec State Park. "Sullivan," Boone said, "This is the region I was telling you about. In these hills you'll find copper, lead, and game in abundance."

Sullivan and his wife settled there. His son was mentioned by Jesse James as having the best horses in the area. Over the years, Route 66 and the Frisco railroad came through, bringing prosperity to the area.

The Meramec State Park, located just outside Sullivan, includes almost 7000 acres of land and adjoins the wilderness of Washington County. In the mid 1970s, Missouri's own bigfoot creature, nicknamed "MoMo" by the local press, was reportedly sighted in the forests of Meramec State Park. Sightings of the Missouri Monster are still reported every few years.

When I was a high school student, the haunted tombstone at the Crow cemetery on Seminary Rd. was the local scare for the kids. One stone, turned slightly different from the others, would glow with its own eerie light.

This was the first ghost hunt I was ever on. In 1980, I drove out to the cemetery with friends, and saw the glow myself. Having been scared by the legends and my own fertile imagination, I managed to stand my ground, and figured out that due to its position, the headlights would shine on it as they made the curve on Seminary Road over a quarter of a mile away. Today, the legends of the ghostly stone in the cemetery still haunt the internet and the caretakers of the graveyard have had to place a fence there to discourage vandals from driving into it at night.

Beyond the Shadows

I was proud, considering this was my first ghost hunt and a successful one as I managed to prove it was not a real ghost.

General William Harney made quite a name for himself. One of the names given to him was "Man who runs like a deer", bestowed on him by Crow Indians he used to challenge to races. He had fought pirate Gene LaFitte and, in the Seminole War and had chased Gen. Santa Ana in the Southwest, working with such notable men as Capt. Abe Lincoln. Harney was captured by the Confederates and taken to Gen. Lee, who offered him a command with the rebel army. After Harney refused, Lee respected him enough to have Harney escorted to Washington D.C., his original destination.

After the war, Harney bought a home in Sullivan. It had been built in 1856 by Dr. Leffingwell. Harney added to the building, using the same style and native stone as was originally used. In 1872, it became his summer home. He moved in 1884, and the mansion went through a series of hands until it stood empty for many years. It fell into a state of disrepair, and was condemned. A group of civic minded citizens around Sullivan formed a group to save the mansion. While they managed to keep it from falling under the bulldozer treads, they could not keep out the vandals or the kids who were using it for parties.

The Harney Foundation formed a number of years ago and are working to restore the building, possibly for use as a library and civic center. Recently, Missouri Paranormal Research went inside to investigate the same rumors of haunting that I had heard as a student in the 80s.

Tim Clifton, senior investigator with MPR, invited me along. However, I was on an investigation in Berger, and was unable to attend. He did tell me of several experiences, including the odor of honeysuckle during an EVP session, and the smell of cigar smoke during another session. They also reported hearing footsteps upstairs while everyone was accounted for, and the mansion was locked down.

On Saturday, July 21, I got my chance. Tim Clifton invited me along for a follow-up investigation. As you approach the mansion, it appears to be in excellent condition.

When you get close, however, you'll notice the windows and doors, including the old style keyhole locks, are merely painted on the plywood covering the windows and doors.

Inside, the gravel and dirt floors attest to the damage done by vandals over the years. "The Friends of the General Harney House" have done a lot to rebuild the mansion, tuck pointing and putting on a new roof to stop the deterioration. One room has some replicas of old furniture in an attempt to recapture the feel of the house from its glory days. However, replacing the wood floor alone has been estimated to cost $1.5 million.

While MPR sensitives believed they were in contact with several spirits, I found very little in the Harney section. After a lockdown, during which video and audio cameras were turned on and all living people were out of the mansion, we went back inside and Tim and I investigated the Leffingwell section of the house.

Here, we felt cold chills and winds where there should not have been any. Photos taken showed an abnormal amount of orbs, and voices could be heard. I felt a light touch, and orbs were photographed around me at that moment. One orb continued to stay behind me, no matter which way I turned in an attempt to face the spirit.

Meanwhile, upstairs, MPR investigators had plaster thrown at them by unseen hands, and a weight on a string began swinging wildly for no reason. Some photos taken showed strange lights and one taken by Spookstalker showed a large, glowing orb on the back porch during the lockdown. A photo taken by Tim Clifton showed what appears to be boney fingers coming from a white mist around the ankle of one of the investigators. This same investigator complained of something grabbing him by the leg later in the night, upstairs.

43

Beyond the Shadows

The mansion may very well be haunted, possibly by Gen. Harney, along with others. Every October, a celebration is held on the grounds of the mansion which includes Civil War reenactors and tours of the building complete with period costumes and furniture.

That will provide you with an opportunity to see the building, and look for the ghosts yourself.

Ask yourself this question first -- is the ghostly smell of a cigar considered second-hand smoke?

Photo by Tim Clifton

Unexplained energy showed up in this photo taken in the old Leffingwell side of the Harney Mansion.

**"She was a phantom of delight
When first she gleamed upon my sight;
A lovely apparition, sent
To be a moment's ornament."
William Wordsworth**

Exploring the Ghosts of Franklin County

Photo by Tim Clifton

A mist surrounds an investigator's leg in the Harney Mansion. Later he felt something grab his leg.

"There is a fatality, a feeling so irrestible and inevitable that it has the force of doom, which almost invariably compels human beings to linger around and haunt, ghostlike, the spot where some great and marked event has given the color to their lifetime; and still the more irrestistibly, the darker the tinge that saddens it."
Nathaniel Hawthorne

Beyond the Shadows

Chapter 8

More Shadows to Explore
"no matter where you go, there they are"

In Franklin County, there are still a few stories circulating, but I have not been able to locate witnesses to them. I place them here for your information only.

Anaconda Cemetery: Located between Stanton and St. Clair near I-44, Anaconda is a quiet community with no commerce. At one time, it was a bustling village with a community church, railroad station, stockyards, general store, blacksmith shop, and other businesses. All of that is gone. All that remains are a few homes, a Baptist church, and a school for special needs children.

Anaconda Cemetery sits on a hill overlooking I-44. A large, dead tree in the center gives a gothic look to the scene. Night time cemetery hunts there have resulted in strange photos including orbs, shadows, and human shapes.

One person reported going there at night, and being attacked by an old woman slamming her hands on the car windshield and demanding to know what he wanted. Then, she ran a few steps away and disappeared. Due to vandalism, a fence was erected to keep out nightly visitors. Should the fence be taken down? Maybe the vandals could do with a visit from the ghostly guard.

Meramec Caverns: Rumors of ghosts inside the cave were abundant when I worked there in the 80s. Older guides, long gone to other jobs, reported seeing a lady in white walking in the upper levels, and Indians in the lower levels walking past the tours. Even recent employees have told me of strange feelings and sightings of the founder, Lester Dill, still in his office.

Beyond the Shadows

<u>Glaser Rd.</u> Just outside Sullivan, Glaser Road is a back road running from Sullivan to Stanton. Rumors were of a green mist or blob, which floated in the woods. Even teachers reported seeing this back in the 50s and 60s. No one has reported seeing it since.

<u>Elijah McLean's:</u> A former restaurant in Washington, it overlooks the Missouri River. Several former employees have told me of weird feelings and seeing objects move. One former resident, when the building was turned into apartments, said he saw the spirit of a mother, father and small girl. This resident also had objects thrown at him.

The restaurant is closed now. The owner has not allowed us inside to investigate.

<u>Old Highway 100:</u> Running between Gray Summit and Washington, there have been reports of a hitchhiking ghost thumbing rides into Washington. Just outside the city limits, he disappears. Could this be one of the ghosts inside the old Diamonds?

And there are others. Franklin County has a rich history and a bright future. At night, however, the county takes on another kind of night life, unseen by most people. I have spoken to many people who do not speak of the ghosts, but live with them. In most cases, the two different types of inhabitants ignore each other, and the living just live with the ghostly company. Who is watching you at night?

Exploring the Ghosts of Franklin County

Photo by Dan Terry

A milky orb inside a milk crate in the basement of Darlene's One Stop in Berger.

Beyond the Shadows

Photo by Jamie Eckerle
The figure of a ghost can be discerned outside this window of the Hall Hotel in Berger.

"Our revels now are ended. These our actors,
As I foretold you, were all spirits and:
Are melted into air, into thin air:
And, like the baseless fabric of this vision,
The cloud-capp'd towers, the gorgeous palaces,
The solemn temples, the great globe itself,
Yea, all which it inherit, shall dissolve
And, like this insubstantial pageant faded,
Leave not a rack behind. We are such stuff
As dreams are made of, and our little life
Is rounded with a sleep."
--William Shakespeare